Date: 3/21/17

BR 398.2 HIL
Hillert, Margaret,
Margaret Hillert's the funny
baby /

The Funny Baby

DEAR CAREGIVER,

The books in this Beginning-to-Read collection may look somewhat familiar in that the original versions could have been a part of your own early reading experiences. These carefully written texts feature common sight words to provide your child multiple exposures to the words appearing most frequently in written text. These new versions have been updated and the engaging illustrations are highly appealing to a contemporary audience of young readers.

Begin by reading the story to your child, followed by letting him or her read familiar words and soon your child will be able to read the story independently. At each step of the way, be sure to praise your reader's efforts to build his or her confidence as an independent reader. Discuss the pictures and encourage your child to make connections between the story and his or her own life. At the end of the story, you will find reading activities and a word list that will help your child practice and strengthen beginning reading skills. These activities, along with the comprehension questions are aligned to current standards, so reading efforts at home will directly support the instructional goals in the classroom.

Above all, the most important part of the reading experience is to have fun and enjoy it!

Shannon Cannon

Shannon Cannon,
Literacy Consultant

Norwood House Press • www.norwoodhousepress.com
Beginning-to-Read™ is a registered trademark of Norwood House Press.
Illustration and cover design copyright ©2017 by Norwood House Press. All Rights Reserved.

Authorized adapted reprint from the U.S. English language edition, entitled The Funny Baby by Margaret Hillert. Copyright © 2017 Pearson Education, Inc. or its affiliates. Reprinted with permission. All rights reserved. Pearson and The Funny Baby are trademarks, in the US and/or other countries, of Pearson Education, Inc. or its affiliates. This publication is protected by copyright, and prior permission to re-use in any way in any format is required by both Norwood House Press and Pearson Education. This book is authorized in the United States for use in schools and public libraries.

Designer: Lindaanne Donohoe
Editorial Production: Lisa Walsh

LIBRARY OF CONGRESS CATALOGING-IN-PUBLICATION DATA
Names: Hillert, Margaret, author. | Wendland, Paula Zinngrabe, illustrator. | Andersen, H. C. (Hans Christian), 1805-1875. Grimme Ulling.
Title: The funny baby / by Margaret Hillert ; illustrated by Paula Wendland.
Description: Chicago, IL : Norwood House Press, 2016. | Series: A beginning-to-read book | Summary: "An easy format retelling of the classic fairy tale, The Ugly Duckling who turns into a beautiful swan. Original edition revised with new illustrations. Includes reading activities and a word list"-- Provided by publisher.
Identifiers: LCCN 2015047806 (print) | LCCN 2016014752 (ebook) | ISBN 9781599537818 (library edition : alk. paper) | ISBN 9781603579223 (eBook)
Subjects: | CYAC: Fairy tales.
Classification: LCC PZ8.H5425 Fu 2016 (print) | LCC PZ8.H5425 (ebook) | DDC [E]--dc23
LC record available at http://lccn.loc.gov/2015047806

288N—072016
Manufactured in the United States of America in North Mankato, Minnesota.

Margaret Hillert's

The Funny Baby

A Beginning-to-Read Book

Illustrated by Paula Wendland
retold story of The Ugly Duckling

NORWOOD HOUSE PRESS

Oh, look.
Here is something.
One little one.
Two little ones.
Three little ones.
And a big one.

Where is the mother?
Can you find the mother?

See here.
Here is the mother.
See mother go.

Look, look.
Mother is here.

Oh, my. Oh, my.
Look in here.
One little one.
Two little ones.
Three little ones.

And—
One big one!

One yellow one.
Two yellow ones.
Three yellow ones.

And—
One is not yellow!
It is not my baby.

Away we go.
We can play.
It is fun to play.

Here I come.
Here I come.
I want to play.

16

Not you, not you.
You look funny.
Go away.
You can not play.

Oh my, oh my.
I look funny.
I can not play.

I look funny.
I can not help it.
Where can I go?

Away I go.
Away, away, away.

Look up here.
Something is yellow.
Something is red.

Oh, oh, oh.
Look down here.
It is not fun.
Help me. Help me.

Look, look!
See me.
Oh, my!
Away I go!

Look in here.
See me.
It is fun.

Look, look!
Oh, my.
I see something.
Something big.

Oh, oh, oh.
Look down here.
See me.
See me.
See big, big me.

Away we go!
Away, away, away.

Foundational Skills

In addition to reading the numerous high-frequency words in the text, this book also supports the development of foundational skills.

Phonological Awareness: The /u/ sound

Sound Substitution: Say the words on the left to your child. Ask your child to repeat the word, changing the middle sound to /**u**/:

fin = fun	cap = cup	mad = mud	bat = but
lick = luck	dig = dug	shot = shut	rib = rub
fizz = fuzz	track = truck	bin = bun	rag = rug
snag = snug	lamp = lump	stamp = stump	

Phonics: The letter Uu

1. Demonstrate how to form the letters **U** and **u** for your child.
2. Have your child practice writing **U** and **u** at least three times each.
3. Ask your child to point to the words in the book that have the letter **u** in them.
4. Write down the following words and ask your child to circle the letter **u** in each word:

you	fluff	funny	run	loud	duck
bus	sound	fur	nut	shut	caught
up	such	under	round	plump	pup

Fluency: Shared Reading

1. Reread the story to your child at least two more times while your child tracks the print by running a finger under the words as they are read. Ask your child to read the words he or she knows with you.
2. Reread the story taking turns, alternating readers between sentences or pages.

Language

The concepts, illustrations, and text help children develop language both explicitly and implicitly.

Vocabulary: Adjectives

1. Explain to your child that words that describe something are called adjectives.
2. Say the following adjectives and ask your child to name something that the adjective might describe:

funny	little	tall	short	cuddly	pretty
big	silly	cute	noisy	furry	soft

3. Write the words on sticky note paper.
4. Read each word aloud for your child.
5. Mix the words up randomly and say each word to your child. Ask your child to point to the correct word.

Reading Literature and Informational Text

To support comprehension, ask your child the following questions. The answers either come directly from the text or require inferences and discussion.

Key Ideas and Detail

- Ask your child to retell the sequence of events in the story.
- Why did the mother think the big baby wasn't hers?

Craft and Structure

- Is this a book that tells a story or one that gives information? How do you know?
- How do you think the funny baby felt when he could not play?

Integration of Knowledge and Ideas

- What happened to the funny baby?
- What is the lesson in the story?

WORD LIST

The Funny Baby uses the 40 words listed below.

This list can be used to practice reading the words that appear in the text. You may wish to write the words on index cards and use them to help your child build automatic word recognition. Regular practice with these words will enhance your child's fluency in reading connected text.

a	go	not	up
and			
away	help	oh	want
	here	one(s)	we
baby			where
big	I	play	
	in		yellow
can	is	red	you
come	it		
		see	
down	little	something	
	look		
find		the	
fun	me	three	
funny	Mother	to	
	my	two	

ABOUT THE AUTHOR   Margaret Hillert has helped millions of children all over the world learn to read independently. She was a first grade teacher for 34 years and during that time started writing books that her students could both gain confidence in reading and enjoy. She wrote well over 100 books for children just learning to read. As a child, she enjoyed writing poetry and continued her poetic writings as an adult for both children and adults.

Photograph by Glenna Washburn

ABOUT THE ILLUSTRATOR   Paula Wendland grew up in Illinois, where both of her parents were artists and so her education as an artist began early. She went on to achieve professional training, graduating with a BA in Art and English and a diploma from the School of the Museum of Fine Arts in Boston. She's always enjoyed reading and illustrating folktales. She thinks that's because folktales inhabit a fantastical world on the cusp between reality and imagination, and anything can happen!